D0549264

This book belongs to

....

....

WALTHAM FOREST LIBRARIES

904 000 00670060

For Joe, Thea and Tom and Ed – EK

Special thanks to Gussie – LDB

WALTHAM FOREST
LIBRARIES

904 000 00670060

| Askews & Holts | 07-Aug-2020 |
| JF PIC | |

Published by Little Door Books 2020
This edition published 2020
ISBN: 978-1-9999556-3-2
Text and Illustrations copyright © Esther Kent 2020
The right of Esther Kent to be identified as author and illustrator of this work has been asserted in accordance with the Copyright, Designs and Patents Act 1988.

All rights reserved. No part of this publication may be reproduced, stored in a retrieval system, or transmitted in any form or by any means, electronic, mechanical, photocopying, recording or otherwise, without prior permission of the publishers.
A CIP catalogue record for this book is available from the British Library.

Little Door Books and Little Door Debuts acknowledges support from the National Lottery through Creative Scotland towards the publication of this title.

LOTTERY FUNDED

Email: mail@littledoorbooks.co.uk
Website: www.littledoorbooks.co.uk
Twitter: @littledoorbooks, @LDDebuts

Molly's CIRCUS

Esther Kent

There are lots of jobs to do today…

...but I don't mind.

There's a **CIRCUS** in my garden.

Here's a washing line high wire

clowns carrying water

bicycles, tricycles and unicycles!

Trapeze
in the trees

feathery acrobats

balancing high

And I am Molly,

Ringmaster Extraordinaire!

I tell mum everything.

She says,

Oh Molly!

Everyday is a CIRCUS with you around.